KU-393-736

A Midsummer Night's Dream

A Shakespeare Story

RETOLD BY ANDREW MATTHEWS
ILLUSTRATED BY TONY ROSS

ORCHARD BOOKS

To Hannah, love you more than...
A.M.

For Laura K.
T.R.

ORCHARD BOOKS
96 Leonard Street, London EC2A 4XD
Orchard Books Australia
Unit 31/56 O'Riordan Street, Alexandria NSW 2015
This text was first published in Great Britain in the form of
a gift collection called *The Orchard Book of Shakespeare Stories,*
illustrated by Angela Barrett in 2001.
This edition first published in hardback in Great Britain in 2002
First paperback publication 2003
Text © Andrew Matthews 2001
Illustrations © Tony Ross 2002
The rights of Andrew Matthews to be identified as the author and
Tony Ross as the illustrator of this work have been asserted by them
in accordance with the Copyright, Designs, and Patents Act, 1988.
ISBN 1 84121 316 0 (hardback)
ISBN 1 84121 332 2 (paperback)
1 3 5 7 9 10 8 6 4 2 (hardback)
1 3 5 7 9 10 8 6 4 2 (paperback)
A CIP catalogue record for this book is available
from the British Library.
Printed in Great Britain

Contents

Cast List

Hermia

In love with Lysander

Helena

Friend to Hermia
In love with Demetrius

Demetrius

Betrothed to Hermia

Lysander

In love with Hermia

Oberon

King of the Fairies

Titania

Queen of the Fairies

Puck

An Elf

Bottom

A Weaver

The Scene

In and around Athens, Ancient Greece.

Ay me, for aught that I could ever read,
Could ever hear by tale or history,
The course of true love never did run smooth,

Lysander; I.i.

A Midsummer Night's Dream

When the path of true love runs smoothly, the world seems a wonderful place – all bright skies and smiling faces.

Unfortunately, true love has a habit of wandering off the path and getting lost, and when that happens people's lives get lost too, in a tangle of misery.

Take the love of Duke Theseus of Athens and Hippolyta, Queen of the Amazons, for instance. They were to be married, and their happiness spread through the whole of Athens. People had decorated their houses with flowers, and left lamps burning in their windows at night, so that the streets twinkled like a

city of stars. Everybody was joyful and excited as they prepared to celebrate the Duke's wedding day. Well, almost everybody…

✳ ✳ ✳

On the day before the royal wedding, two friends met by chance in the market square: golden-haired Hermia, and black-haired Helena, both beautiful and both with secrets that made their hearts ache.

For a while, the two friends chatted about nothing in particular. Then Helena noticed a look in Hermia's deep blue eyes that made her ask, "Is everything all right, Hermia?"

Hermia looked so sad and serious.

"I am to marry Demetrius tomorrow," she replied.

"Demetrius!" said Helena softly. Now her heart was aching worse than ever. Night after night she had cried herself to sleep, whispering Demetrius's name, knowing that her love for him was hopeless.  Many years ago the families of Hermia and Demetrius had agreed that, when they were of age, their daughter and son should marry. "You must be the happiest young woman in Athens!" sighed Helena.

"I've never been so miserable in my life!" Hermia declared. "You see, I don't love Demetrius."

"You don't?" cried Helena, amazed.

"I'm in love with Lysander," Hermia confessed, and she began to describe all the things that made Lysander so wonderful.

Helena thought about Lysander, with his curly brown hair and broad smile. He was *quite* handsome, she supposed, but he didn't have Demetrius's dark, brooding good looks. Why on earth did Hermia find him so attractive?

"Of course, I told my father that I didn't wish to marry Demetrius," Hermia said, "and he went straight to him to explain – but you know how stubborn Demetrius can be. He lost his temper and said it didn't matter who I loved, our marriage had been arranged and it must go ahead, no matter what. His stupid pride's been hurt, that's all – he doesn't love me a bit."

"Then who does he love?" Helena enquired eagerly.

"No one, except for himself," said Hermia. "I *can't* marry someone I don't love, and I know it will cause a scandal, but Lysander and I are going to run away together!"

"*When*?" Helena asked.

"Tonight," Hermia told her. "I'm meeting him at midnight in the wood outside the city walls. We plan to travel through the night, and in the morning we'll find a little temple where we can be married. Oh, Helena, it will be so *romantic*! Please say that you're happy for me!"

"Of course I am," said Helena. "I'm overjoyed."

And she was overjoyed – for herself. 'At last, this is my chance!' she thought.

'If I visit Demetrius tonight and tell him that Hermia and Lysander have gone off together, he'll forget about his pride...and then...when I tell him how I feel about him, he'll be so flattered, he'll fall in love with me. Love always finds a way!'

Which is true, but love doesn't always find the way that people expect, as Helena was about to find out. For it was not only in the human world that love was causing unhappiness; although Helena and Hermia did not know it, two different worlds would meet in the wood outside Athens that night, and the result would be chaos.

✳ ✳ ✳

Oberon, King of
the Fairies, was
a creature of
darkness and
shadows, while his
wife, Queen Titania,
was moonlight and
silver. The two loved each

other dearly, but they had quarrelled
bitterly. Titania had taken
a little orphan boy as a
page, and made such
a fuss of the lad
that Oberon
had become
very jealous.
He wanted
the page
for himself.

That midsummer's night, in a clearing in the wood, Titania was singing to her page, while fairy servants fluttered around her like glittering moths.

When Oberon appeared, Titania's silvery eyes darkened. "Fairies, let us leave this place at once!" she said haughtily.

"Wait, Titania!" snapped Oberon. "This quarrel of ours has gone on long enough. You say I have no reason to be jealous of the boy – very well, prove it! Give him to me!"

"Not for all your fairy kingdom!" hissed Titania. She raised her left hand, and sent a ball of blue fire roaring across the glade, straight at Oberon's head.

Oberon spoke a word of magic, and the fire turned to water that burst over him, drenching his clothes. By the time he had rubbed the water from his eyes, the glade was empty and Oberon was alone. "I'll make you sorry for this, Titania!" he vowed. Then, lifting his dripping head, he called out, "Puck? Come to me, now!"

A breeze sighed in the branches, as an elf dropped out of the air and landed at Oberon's feet. The elf was dressed in leaves that had been sewn together. His hair was tangled, his skin as brown as chestnuts, and when he smiled, his white teeth flashed mischievously. "Command me, master!" Puck said.

"I mean to teach the Queen a lesson," said Oberon. "Go, search the Earth and fetch me the flower called Love in Idleness."

"I will fly faster than a falling star!" said Puck, and with that he had vanished.

A cruel smile played on Oberon's lips. "When Titania is asleep, I will drop the juice of the flower in her eyes," he said to himself. "Its magic will make her fall in love with the first living thing she sees when she wakes – perhaps a toad, or even a spider! She will make herself seem so ridiculous, that she will beg me to break the spell, and I will...after she's given me the page!"

This plan pleased Oberon so much that he began to laugh – but his laugh was cut short when he heard human voices approaching. With a wave of his fingers, Oberon made himself vanish among the shadows.

✳ ✳ ✳

Demetrius, out searching for Hermia, halted in the middle of the glade, while he considered which path to take. This gave Helena a chance to catch up with him. "Wait for me, Demetrius!" she pleaded.

Demetrius scowled at her. "For the last time, Helena, go home!" he shouted angrily. "I can find Lysander and Hermia without your help."

"But you don't understand!" Helena exclaimed. "I love you! I've always loved you!"

She tried to put her arms around Demetrius, but he ducked away. "Well I don't love you!" he said roughly. "So go away and leave me alone!"

And he ran off through the moonlight.

"Oh, Demetrius!" sobbed Helena, running after him. "I would follow you through fire, just to be near you!"

* * *

When the glade was once more still and
silent, Oberon came out of the darkness.
His face was thoughtful. "I must help that
lovely maiden!" he whispered. "I know
how cruel it is to love someone whose
heart is so cold."

A wind brushed the Fairy King's cheek,
and there stood Puck, holding a sprig of
glimmering white flowers.

"Take two blossoms and search the woods for a young human couple," Oberon said to him. "Squeeze the juice of the petals into the young man's eyes, but do it when you are sure that the maiden will be the first thing he sees."

"At once, master!" Puck said with a bow, and then he was gone.

Then Oberon went to find Titania.
He found her sleeping alone on a bank of
violets, and the air was heavy with their
sweet perfume. As he dropped juice from
the magic flowers on to Titania's eyelids,
Oberon murmured:

"What you see when you awake,
Do it for your true love take!"

* * *

At that very moment, in another part of the wood, Puck was putting magic juice into the eyes of a young man he had found sleeping next to a young woman at the foot of a pine tree.

"When he wakes and sees her, his love for her will drive him mad!" Puck giggled, and he leapt into the air, like a grasshopper in a summer meadow.

But, as bad luck would have it, Puck had found the wrong couple. Those sleeping under the tree were Lysander and Hermia, who had got lost in the wood and exhausted themselves trying to find the way out.

And as bad luck would also have it, a few seconds after Puck had left them, Helena wandered by, searching for Demetrius. Blinded by tears, Helena did not notice Lysander and Hermia until she stumbled over Lysander's legs.

He woke, saw her, and his eyes bulged like a frog's as the magic went to work.

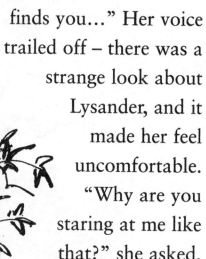

"Lysander?" gasped Helena. "What are you doing here? I mean, you mustn't be here! Get away quickly! Demetrius is looking for you, and if he finds you..." Her voice trailed off – there was a strange look about Lysander, and it made her feel uncomfortable. "Why are you staring at me like that?" she asked.

"Because at last I have found my own true love," said Lysander. "Helena, can't you see how much I love you?"

Helena stepped back, laughing nervously. "Don't be silly, Lysander!" she said. "You love Hermia...don't you?"

"Hermia, who is she?" scoffed Lysander, scrambling to his feet. "How could I love anyone but you, with your eyes like stars, your hair as black as ravens' wings, and your skin as soft as...?"

"That's quite enough of that!" said
Helena. "This is some sort of midsummer
madness!"

"Madness? Yes, I'm mad!" said
Lysander. "Mad with love for you!
Come to my arms, and cool the fires
of my passion with your kisses!"

He moved towards Helena, but she
turned and fled. Lysander followed her,
shouting, "There's no escape from love,
Helena! This was meant to be!"

Their loud voices and pounding footsteps woke Hermia. "Lysander, where are you?" she muttered sleepily. "Don't wander off on your own, my love. You might be eaten by a lion, or a bear…" The very thought made her wide awake, and she sat up. "Or I might be eaten, come to that!" she said with a shudder. "I'm coming to find you, Lysander, so we can be eaten together!"

＊ ＊ ＊

Not five paces from the bank of
violets where Titania lay asleep, a group
of Athenians had gathered in secret to
rehearse a play that they meant to perform
for Duke Theseus after his wedding. One
of the actors, a weaver called Bottom, was
behind a tree, waiting to appear
when he heard his cue.

"I'll show them how
it's done!" Bottom
said to himself.
"When the Duke
sees what a fine
actor I am, he'll
give me a purse
of gold, or my
name's not
Nick Bottom!"

He glanced up,
and saw a strange
orange light
circling the tree.
"Now what's
that, I wonder?"
he muttered.
"A firefly
perhaps?"

It was Puck.
He had noticed
the actors as he
flew by on his
way back to
Oberon, and had seen
a chance to make mischief.
"Behold, the Queen's new love!" he said.
Magic sparks showered down from his
fingertips on to the weaver.

Immediately Bottom's face began to sprout hair, and his nose and ears grew longer and longer. His body was unchanged, so Bottom had no idea that anything was wrong, until he heard his cue and stepped out from behind a tree.

Bottom had meant his entrance to be dramatic, and it certainly was. The other actors took one look at the donkey-headed monster coming towards them, and raced away screaming and shouting.

"What's the matter with them?" said Bottom, scratching his chin. "My word, my beard has grown quickly today! I'll need a good shave before the performance tomorrow!" He paced this way and that, puzzling out why his friends had left in such a hurry. "O-o-h! I see-haw, hee-haw!" he said at last. "They're trying to frighten me by leaving me alone in the wood in the dark! Well it won't work! It takes more than that to frighten a man like me-haw, hee-haw!"

And to prove how brave he was, Bottom began to sing. His voice was part human, part donkey and it sounded like the squealing of rusty hinges. It woke Queen Titania from her sleep on the bank of violets. "Do I hear an angel singing?" she said, and raised herself on one elbow and gazed at Bottom. "Adorable human, I have fallen wildly in love with you!" she told him.

"Really?" said Bottom, not the least alarmed by the sudden appearance of the Fairy Queen. He was sure it was all part of the trick his friends were playing.

"Sit beside me, so I can stroke your long, silky ears!" Titania purred. "My servants will bring you anything you desire."

"I wouldn't say no to some supper," said Bottom. "Nothing fancy – a bale of hay or a bag of oats would suit me fine!"

From up above came the sound of Puck's laughter, like the pealing of tiny bells.

❋ ❋ ❋

Oberon's laughter set every owl in the wood hooting. "My proud Queen, in love with a donkey?" he cried. "Well done, Puck! Titania will think twice before she defies me again! But what of the humans?"

"I did as you commanded, master," said
Puck. "I found them…"

A voice made him turn his head, and he
saw Demetrius stamping along the path,
dragging Hermia by the arm.

"That is the fellow!" said Oberon. "But
who is that with him?"

"He is not the one I cast the spell on!"
Puck yelped.

"Quickly," said Oberon. "Make
yourself invisible before they see us!"

✳ ✳ ✳

Hermia was thoroughly miserable.
Everything had gone wrong: she had
found Demetrius instead of Lysander, and
Demetrius was in such a foul temper that
she feared the worst. "Oh, where is
Lysander?" she wailed. "You've killed
him, haven't you, you brute?"

With a weary groan, Demetrius let Hermia go and slumped to the ground. "I haven't touched your precious Lysander!" he yawned. "Now stop whining and get some sleep. When it's light, we'll find our way out of this accursed wood."

"I won't rest until I find Lysander!" Hermia said defiantly.

"Just as you wish," said Demetrius. "I'm too tired to argue any more."

He lay back among the ferns and closed his eyes. He heard Hermia walking away, and then he fell into a deep sleep.

Moonlight shifted and shivered as Oberon and Puck reappeared. "This is the man," said Oberon, peering down at Demetrius. "Search the wood for a black-haired maiden, and bring her here. When she is close by I will put magic juice in his eyes and wake him."

"Yes, master! But tell me, is human love always so complicated?" Puck asked curiously.

"Just do as I have commanded!" snapped Oberon.

✳ ✳ ✳

Helena was still running, with Lysander just a few steps behind her. So many bewildering things had happened to her, that when an orange light appeared above the path in front of her, she was not surprised – in fact, a curious idea suddenly popped into her mind – Puck's magic had put it there. Helena became convinced that if she followed the light, it would lead her

back to Athens, and sanity. Over streams and through clearings the light led her, until at last she came to a deep thicket of ferns, where she paused for breath.

"Helena, marry me!" she heard Lysander shout.

"I don't want you!" she shouted back. "I want Demetrius!"

"And here I
am my love!"
said Demetrius,
springing up out
of the ferns nearby, his
eyes glowing with magic.
"Hold me, let me melt in your sweetness!"
Helena did not bother to wonder why
Demetrius had changed his mind: her
dreams had come true, and she was about

to rush into his arms
when Lysander ran
between them.
"Keep away
from her,
Demetrius!"
Lysander
said hotly.
"Helena is mine!"

"Lysander...is that you?" called a voice, and Hermia came stumbling out of the bushes. Brambles had torn the hem of her dress, and there were leaves and twigs stuck in her hair. "Thank the gods you're safe!" she said, weeping for joy. "Why did you leave me, my only love?"

"Because I can't bear the sight of you!" said Lysander. "I want to marry Helena."

"So do I!" Demetrius exclaimed. "And since she can't marry both of us, we'll have to settle the matter, man to man!"

He pushed Lysander's chest, knocking him backwards, then Lysander pushed Demetrius.

Hermia stared at Helena, her eyes blazing. "You witch! You've stolen my Lysander!" she screeched.

"I haven't stolen anybody!" Helena replied angrily. "This is all some cruel trick, isn't it? The three of you plotted together to make a fool of me – and I thought you were my friend!"

"Our friendship ended when you took Lysander away from me!" snarled Hermia.

And there might have been a serious fight, if Oberon had not cast a sleeping spell on all four of them. They dropped to the ground like ripe apples, Hermia falling close to Lysander and Helena collapsing at Demetrius's side.

Oberon and
Puck appeared
magically
beside them.
"Smear their eyes
with fairy juice!"
said Oberon. "This knot
of lovers will unravel when they wake."

As Puck hurried about his task, the air
was filled with the singing of fairy voices.
"The Queen!" Puck muttered in alarm.
"The Queen is coming!"

* * *

Titania did not notice Puck and Oberon, or
the sleeping lovers. She could see nothing
but Bottom, whose jaws were stretched
open in a wide yawn. "Are you weary,
dearest one?" she asked him tenderly. "Rest
with me on these soft ferns."

"I feel a powerful sleep coming over me-haw, hee-haw!" said Bottom.

"Fairies, leave us!" ordered Titania.

The fairies flew away, leaving bright trails in the air. Titania cradled Bottom's head in her lap, and they both dozed.

Oberon and Puck crept close. Puck began to grin, but he stopped when he saw the sorrow in his master's eyes.

"There is no laughter in this!" Oberon sighed. "How I long for Titania to smile at me, as she smiled at this creature, and to feel her soft arms around me as I sleep! Break the spell on the human, Puck, while I deal with the Queen."

Oberon moved his hands, weaving shadows into magic as he chanted:

"Be the way you used to be,
See the way you used to see,
Wake, my Queen, and come to me!"

Titania opened her eyes, and when she saw Oberon she flew into his arms. "I am so glad that you are here, my love!" she said. "I had the strangest dream! I dreamed that I had fallen in love with a..."

"We will never quarrel again," Oberon promised. "Keep your page – have fifty pages if you wish! What does it matter, as long as we are together?"

Puck saw that the sky was getting lighter. "It's almost dawn, master!" he warned.

"Then we must leave!" said Oberon, and he, Titania and Puck faded into the pale morning light.

When the sun rose, its light woke
Demetrius and Helena, who fell in love at
first sight, then Lysander and Hermia,
who fell in love all over again. There was
much smiling, sighing and kissing, and
soon Demetrius said, "Today is Duke
Theseus's wedding day, as well as mine
and Helena's. Come, my friends, the priest
can marry us all at the same ceremony!"

And the lovers hurried off towards
Athens, laughing every step of the way,
the paths of their true love running
smoothly at last.

∗ ∗ ∗

And as for Bottom, he woke some time
later and clambered stiffly to his feet. "I
thought I was…!" He mumbled. "I
thought I had…!" Anxiously, he felt his
face and ears, and then sighed with relief.

"What a midsummer night's dream!" he
exclaimed. "I'll write a poem about it,
and read it to Duke Theseus and his bride,
and the Duke will say: 'Well done, noble
Bottom! Here's some gold for you!'"

And he stumbled away through the
ferns, making up lines of poetry and
reciting them out loud as he went.

The eye of man hath not heard, the ear of man hath not seen, man's hand is not able to taste, his tongue to conceive, nor his heart to report what my dream was.

Bottom; IV.i.

Love and Magic in
A Midsummer Night's Dream

In *A Midsummer Night's Dream* Shakespeare brings together two worlds; the human world of Athens, and the fairy world of the woods outside the city. One world is ruled by law, the other by magic, and in both worlds trouble is brewing.

In the woods outside Athens, Oberon and Titania are busy arguing over a page boy. Meanwhile Demetrius, who is as stubborn as Oberon, is insisting on marrying Hermia, even though she loves someone else. Add a group of bickering actors, and Puck, a mischievous sprite, and madness follows.

The humans are made to love the wrong partners, and Titania falls in love with one of the actors, who has the head of a donkey!

When the human lovers begin to fight one another, the play comes close to tragedy, but magic sets things right. The humans find their true loves and Oberon realises that his love for Titania is stronger than his pride.

The Elizabethans believed in a 'midsummer madness' that was caused by the heat of the summer sun, and many of the characters in *A Midsummer Night's Dream* behave as if they have been touched by this madness.

The fairy world and the human world are thrown into chaos by love, and Shakespeare pokes fun at how lovers behave. And in the character of Bottom he makes fun of actors – and even playwrights like himself too!

Shakespeare and the Globe Theatre

Some of Shakespeare's most famous plays were first performed at the Globe Theatre, which was built on the South Bank of the River Thames in 1599.

Going to the Globe was a different experience from going to the theatre today. The building was roughly circular in shape, but with flat sides: a little like a doughnut crossed with a fifty-pence piece. Because the Globe was an open-air theatre, plays were only put on during daylight hours in spring and summer. People paid a penny to stand in the central space and watch a play, and this part of the audience became known as 'the groundlings' because they stood on the ground. A place in the tiers of seating beneath the thatched roof, where there was a slightly better view and less chance of being rained on, cost extra.

The Elizabethans did not bath very often and the audiences at the Globe were smelly. Fine ladies and gentlemen in the more expensive seats sniffed perfume and bags of sweetly-scented herbs to cover the stink rising from the groundlings.

There were no actresses on the stage; all the female characters in Shakespeare's plays would have been acted by boys, wearing wigs and make-up. Audiences were not well-behaved. People clapped and cheered when their favourite actors came on stage; bad actors were jeered at and sometimes pelted with whatever came to hand.

Most Londoners worked hard to make a living and in their precious free time they liked to be entertained. Shakespeare understood the magic of the theatre so well that today, almost four hundred years after his death, his plays still cast a spell over the thousands of people that go to see them.

Orchard Classics
Shakespeare Stories

RETOLD BY ANDREW MATTHEWS
ILLUSTRATED BY TONY ROSS

A Midsummer Night's Dream	ISBN 1 84121 332 2	£3.99
Antony and Cleopatra	ISBN 1 84121 338 1	£3.99
Hamlet	ISBN 1 84121 340 3	£3.99
Henry V	ISBN 1 84121 342 X	£3.99
Macbeth	ISBN 1 84121 344 6	£3.99
Romeo and Juliet	ISBN 1 84121 336 5	£3.99
The Tempest	ISBN 1 84121 346 2	£3.99
Twelfth Night	ISBN 1 84121 334 9	£3.99

Orchard Classics are available from all good bookshops,
or can be ordered direct from the publisher:
Orchard Books, PO BOX 29, Douglas IM99 1BQ
Credit card orders please telephone 01624 836000
or fax 01624 837033
or e-mail: bookshop@enterprise.net for details.

To order please quote title, author and ISBN
and your full name and address.
Cheques and postal orders should be
made payable to 'Bookpost plc'.
Postage and packing is FREE within the UK
(overseas customers should add £1.00 per book).

Prices and availability are subject to change.